WALT DISNEY'S

PETER PAN

FAVORITES

Walt Disney's PETER PAN FAVORITES

THE DANBURY PRESS
a division of Grolier Enterprises Inc.

Robert B. Clarke   *Publisher*

Adapted from the Walt Disney motion picture PETER PAN, by arrangement
with The Hospital for Sick Children, London, England; Copyright 1911, 1921
by Charles Scribner's Sons; Copyright 1939 by Lady Cynthia Asquith, Peter L.
Davies, and Barclay's Bank, Ltd.; published 1911 under the title, "Peter Pan
and Wendy," and in 1950 under the title "Peter Pan."

Library of Congress Catalog Card Number 73-3261

Printed in the United States of America   ISBN 0-7172-8108-6

4567890

Introduction

It all started in London, in the bedroom of
Wendy Darling. Wendy was telling stories to
her brothers, John and little Michael, and listening outside her window was Peter Pan! The
four became friends, and Peter returned often
to London to visit and to play with Wendy,
John and Michael. He taught them to fly, and at
night they would leave home to soar over the
city. Fly now with Peter Pan and the Darling
children to the merriest adventures of all.

Table of Contents

Getting Home on Time

Peter Pan often went to London to play with the Darling children in Kensington Gardens. It was getting late one day, so he started back to Never Never Land, and Wendy, John and Michael began walking home.

"It's a long way," said John after a few minutes. "We're going to be late."

"I'm hungry," said Michael. "Tired, too. I wish we were there already."

"Here comes a cab," said Wendy. "Let's go home in that. Then we'll soon be having our supper."

"Good idea," declared John, holding up his umbrella to attract the cab driver's attention. "Hey there, cabby. Stop, please."

The cab driver stopped in answer to John's call. As the children were climbing into the cab, a man in a brown overcoat pushed them aside.

"Never mind those kids, cabby," said the man in brown.
"I'm in a hurry to reach the bank before it closes. Be quick!"

"Yessir," smiled the cabby, thinking the man might tip him better than would the children. "Climb aboard." The man got into the cab, and it trundled away.

"Well," exclaimed Wendy. "That wasn't very nice. The cabby should have taken us. We were first."

"I saw that!" came a shout from on high. It was Peter Pan.

"Peter!" shouted Wendy happily. "I thought you'd gone back to Never Never Land."

"I started out," said Peter, "and then I thought about what *I* was having for supper, and what *you* were having for supper. So I stayed around, hoping for an invitation."

Wendy laughed, then turned serious. "At this rate we'll never get home for supper."

"Never you mind," Peter replied. "I brought along some extra pixie dust. We'll use that to *fly* home."

"Hooray!" yelled the children.

"Now think of a happy thought," Peter said, and soon they were flying swiftly through the air. They soared like birds between buildings and headed for home.

"Yipes!" yelled the cabby when he saw them fly by. "I'm bewitched! I've never seen the likes of that before!" He was so startled, he lost his balance and fell from the driver's seat. THUMP! He landed on the street.

With no driver at the reins the horse started galloping away with the cab. The man in the brown suit had fallen asleep and didn't realize the danger.

Wendy said, "Peter, the horse is running wild. That man could be injured if we don't do something."

"Don't worry," said Peter. "Leave this to me." With a mighty leap he streaked after the cab at top speed. He grabbed the reins and shouted, "Whoa!"

The man inside was now wide awake and shaking with fright. When the cab finally stopped, he scrambled out.

The man mumbled, "I'll go to the bank tomorrow. Money isn't worth all this. I want to get home and into a nice, warm bath!"

"We want to get home, too," laughed the children. They climbed into the cab, and Peter drove them home.

As they were having supper Michael pointed out the window to the lamppost where Peter had tied the horse.

"Good," said Wendy. "The driver found his cab."

"I hope he also found it's better to be fair," said Peter.

The Lost Baton

Wendy, Michael and John, along with Nana, their nursemaid dog, heard some exciting band music, and they ran out of the park to see where it was coming from. Marching along the street was a military band. The soldiers wore big furry hats, smart red jackets and blue pants. In front was a drum major carrying a fancy baton.

Michael was thrilled at the sight. "I hope the drum major throws that baton in the air," he said.

To Michael's delight
the drum major
did just that.
The baton went
twirling upward.
Michael waited
to see it
come down.
But it didn't.
It was stuck
in a tree!

With the band marching behind him, the drum major didn't dare stop. In fact, he didn't even get out of step. He had to keep marching and hope nobody noticed that he had lost his baton. He looked lost with nothing to throw up in the air and catch.

That's why Wendy and the boys were glad to see Peter Pan flying in on the breeze. "Thank goodness you're here," said Wendy, and she told him everything that had happened.

Peter laughed when he heard, and he looked at the tree. He couldn't see the baton, so he flew into the branches. He crawled around and finally found it high in the tree, caught like a pin in a spider web. He grabbed it and glided down to the sidewalk to show it to Wendy, John and Michael.

"I'd love to have this sometime when I'm fighting Captain Hook," Peter said. "I'd use it to bop him left and right and maybe over the head, too." He swung the baton as if it were a baseball bat.

He handed it to John. "Want to hold it?" he asked.

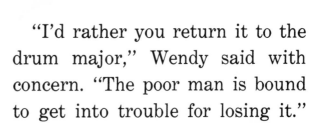

"I'd rather you return it to the drum major," Wendy said with concern. "The poor man is bound to get into trouble for losing it."

"I guess you're right. Leave it to me," replied Peter.

Peter flew away to find the band. He soon spotted the men marching into the military barracks. "I'll try to give this baton back to the drum major without anyone noticing," said Peter.

As Peter flew to the main gate, the drum major was wondering what the colonel would say when he saw the baton was missing. He was very worried. That's why he was so surprised at what happened next.

As the drum major marched through the gate into the barracks square, he heard a funny whistle from above. He glanced up, and Peter tossed down the baton.

Wendy, John and Michael hurried across the park and met Peter near the barracks gate just as the colonel came out to inspect the band.

Wendy asked Peter, "Did you manage to give it back to the drum major in time?"

Peter laughed, "Oh yes. He was so surprised to see it, he nearly dropped it right in front of the colonel."

As it turned out, the colonel was so pleased with the band, he gave the soldiers the rest of the day off.

The drum major went to the park where Peter and the children were playing. "Could I buy each of you some ice cream to show my thanks?" he asked.

Everyone, even Nana the dog, ate ice cream cones while John paraded with the baton, pretending to be a drum major in the army.

Peter Pan exclaimed, "Ice cream makes a fine reward. It pays to be helpful."

"Right," said the drum major. "It pays in more ways than one."

Officer Clump's Revenge

"Good morning, Officer Clump," sang out Wendy Darling. "Will you help me across the street?"

Clump beamed merrily. "Of course, Wendy." He held up his big hand to stop traffic. A car came to a halt, and Wendy walked across the cobblestones.

As she reached the opposite curb, she heard the driver of the car shout, "Seeing children across the street is all you're good for, Clump. You've never arrested anybody or even stopped a runaway horse."

Clump gasped in great dismay. "Oh, Inspector Grubb, please don't talk to me like that. I do my best, really I do."

Inspector Grubb, who was an important police officer, got out of his car and wagged his finger at Clump. "You don't deserve to be a policeman!"

Wendy wanted to help but didn't know how.

While Grubb was talking to Clump, a man jumped in the inspector's car and drove it away!

"I've had my eye on you," Grubb went on. "Unless you do something clever and brave, Clump, I'll fire you."

Suddenly they all realized the car was being stolen. Grubb could hardly believe his eyes. He roared at the top of his voice, "Clump, somebody has stolen my car, and all you can do is stand there doing nothing."

Wendy was feeling very sorry for poor Clump when she heard a quiet voice behind her say, "What's wrong?"

The voice belonged to Peter Pan.

"Oh, Peter, am I glad to see you!" Wendy said. Quickly she told Peter about the stolen car and how Clump was getting all the blame.

Grubb looked down on Clump and said, "It's all your fault, Clump. You're *fired!*" Poor Officer Clump didn't know what to say.

Peter Pan said to Wendy, "If Clump is a friend of yours, I'm going to help him."

Peter turned to the policeman and sprinkled some pixie dust on his helmet. "Think of a happy thought," he said, "and follow me. We'll get the inspector's car back."

"What sort of rubbish is this?" Clump bellowed.

Wendy chimed in, "Do as Peter says, Officer Clump."

Clump was dazed by all that was happening, but he followed Peter into the air. Soon he was flying almost as well as Peter Pan, and he enjoyed soaring above the chimney tops.

"Follow me, Mr. Clump," Peter called, and they set off after the stolen car. When they flew over it, the thief was driving it very fast. Clump slid into the seat beside him and shouted, "Stop this car!"

The thief was so surprised to see Clump sitting beside him that he stopped the car. Not only that, he stopped it in front of the police station.

Clump felt very important as he marched his prisoner inside. "Lock him up, sergeant," said he. "I must take Inspector Grubb's car back to him."

Peter climbed in beside Officer Clump, and off they went. The police officer was very grateful to Peter.

Clump chuckled,
"I don't know how
you worked that
piece of magic,
but I want
to thank you.
You saved my job."

Peter smiled, "Think nothing of it, Mr. Clump. Any friend of Wendy's is a friend of mine."

Later, when Clump had returned the car and explained that the thief was already in jail, Grubb said, "Clump, you're a wonder! I don't know how you did it, but you did. I'm promoting you to sergeant. You're a fine policeman."

Wendy and Peter agreed.

Never Never Land

Some of Peter Pan's adventures took place in London, but some of the most exciting ones happened in Never Never Land. It was easy to get there. When Peter took the Darling children with him, he simply headed for the second star to the right, and straight on till morning.

In Never Never Land Peter was friendly with the Lost Boys, the mermaids, and with the Indian Chief and his daughter, Princess Tiger Lily.

But Never Never Land wasn't all fun. In Cannibal Cove lurked the pirates. Their leader was that villain in silk clothing, Captain Hook. He wore a hook because one day the crocodile bit off his hand. In fact, the croc liked that hand so much it constantly searched for Hook, hoping for the rest of him. The croc also had swallowed an alarm clock, and the tick-tock, tick-tock warned Hook when the croc was near.

Prepare yourself now for Peter's favorite adventures in Never Never Land. Peter also has included some stories about his friends Mowgli and Scamp and Donald Duck.

Read on . . . if you dare!

NEVER NEVER ISLAND

SKULL ROCK

BLINDMAN'S BLUFF

INDIAN CAMP

HANGMAN'S TREE

CROCODILE CREEK

PEGLEG POINT

MERMAID LAGOON

CANNIBAL COVE

N

W

S

E

The Great Race

Captain Hook spent several days in his cabin, thinking, and at last called in Mr. Smee.

"Smee," he exclaimed, "I've got it!"

"Got what, Captain? A headache? A cold in the head?"

"Fool!" Hook bellowed. "I've got a plan to trick Peter Pan and make him my prisoner."

Smee remembered hundreds of other schemes, none of which had worked.

"What's the plan this time?" he asked.

"I'm going to challenge Pan to a race around the island. The loser must leave Never Never Land forever," Hook explained.

Smee felt there was something wrong with the scheme, but he couldn't think what.

Finally Smee figured it out. "But, Captain, I think Peter Pan can run faster than you."

With a snarl the captain pushed his long, bony forefinger into Smee's button nose. "Of course Pan can run faster than I. But after a long race he'll be thirsty, won't he?"

"Certainly," Smee agreed, though he didn't know what he was agreeing with. On the other hand, anything was better than having his nose punched again. "What's your scheme?"

Chuckling wickedly, Hook held up a small bottle, which was filled with a nasty, dark, bad-smelling liquid.

"This bottle is filled with sleeping potion. You will pour this into a glass of lemonade and hand it to Pan after the race," he said.

Hook continued, "Pan will be thirsty, and he will drink all the lemonade. He will then fall asleep, and I will have him in my clutches."

Smee looked worried. "But Pan will know we're up to something crafty if I hand him some lemonade and don't give you some, too."

"You're right for once, Smee," the captain said, scratching his long, pointed chin. "You must have a glass ready for me, too. Now, I'll send my challenge to Peter Pan!"

Peter Pan got the challenge from Captain Hook, and he crowed like a rooster. "Come ahead, Hook. I'll race you — and I'll win!"

Soon the captain and Peter were having their race. At the same time Smee was busy making the lemonade. The first mate filled a large pitcher and then poured in the sleeping potion. He stirred it all up.

Naturally, Peter won the race. When he ran to the finish line, Smee was waiting with a pitcher of lemonade and two glasses.

"You must be thirsty," Smee said, filling both glasses, "so here is some lemonade for you and the captain."

Peter wondered why Smee was there with something to drink. He didn't trust Smee or that tricky captain. Though his throat was dry as dust, Peter slyly threw his lemonade away when Smee wasn't looking.

Captain Hook came puffing over the finish line. "Oh, I'm thirsty," he said. "Let's have something to drink, Smee."

Hook saw that Peter's glass was empty, so he was sure it would be safe to drink the other glass of lemonade.

The captain snatched the glass from Smee and emptied it in a single swallow. Seconds later, a most peaceful expression lit Hook's face. He closed his eyes and slid to the ground. He was snoring loudly by the time he was stretched out.

"What's going on?" Peter asked, staring at the captain and at Smee.

Smee's little eyes grew round. "Y-you d-don't think I p-put a sleeping potion in the l-lemonade, do you?" he stuttered.

"So that was your trick! Hook meant to capture me, eh?"

By the time Captain Hook woke up, Peter was safely hidden in a nearby tree, watching what would happen. Sure enough, there was another race in Never Never Land — with Hook chasing poor Mr. Smee clear around the island.

The Captain's Trousers

Tweeee-eee!

The boatswain's whistle warned the pirate crew that Captain Hook was inspecting their ship for cleanliness. They were nervous because they knew he would be angry if he found dirt anywhere.

Suddenly they heard him roar. A dingy spot on the deck caught his eye. "If this is a smudge," he snarled, bending over to look closely, "I'm going to . . ."

He never finished his sentence. In the middle of it was a loud ripping noise. His trousers split!

How embarrassing! Hook was furious! Quickly he went to his cabin and changed pants. Then he returned to the deck and handed his torn trousers to his first mate, Mr. Smee.

"I want you to sew up the rip. Be quick about it. These are my favorite trousers."

Smee gulped. "Aye, sir. I'll do my best." But he wasn't very good at sewing.

An hour later Smee handed Hook's trousers back to him. "All done, sir. Hope you like it, sir!"

Hook took one look at the trousers and roared, "Terrible! You've ruined them!

"But, sir . . ."

"Out of my sight, nincompoop! I'll get someone else to fix them!" he shouted.

Smee ran below decks to suffer, and Hook began to pace. "Who can I get to-- Say, what about Wendy Darling?"

The pirate said, "Wendy's good at sewing! It was she who sewed on Peter Pan's shadow. Yes, she can fix my trousers."

Hook quickly ordered two of his men to row ashore to capture Wendy.

They returned an hour later, and Hook gloated and rubbed his hands in glee. "I'm so clever that I even amaze myself!"

Soon Wendy was busily sewing Hook's trousers and also some shirts and a torn vest he found in his trunk. When she was finished, he had her scrub the deck!

Meanwhile on the beach, Peter Pan and the Lost Boys were inspecting some strange footprints at their campsite. They had discovered Wendy was missing, and they were being detectives.

John pointed to the footprints.
"I'm sure these were made
by large men wearing sandals,"
he explained carefully.
"Our only men are Indians
and pirates, and only pirates
wear sandals on their feet,"
answered Peter Pan.
"Hook must have captured Wendy."

Peter ran to get his trusty sword. "I'm going to rescue Wendy and teach that rascal Hook a lesson he'll never forget," he cried as he flew into the air.

Moments later Peter zoomed toward the ship. To his surprise he saw Wendy scrubbing the deck. She was being guarded by Mr. Smee and another pirate.

"Enough of this," cried Peter. He rescued Wendy and made the pirates polish the deck. "Oh, Peter, the captain made me fix his trousers and mend his shirt and . . ."

At that moment Hook marched onto the deck!

Seeing Peter,
he bellowed and
rushed forward.
His feet slipped
on the slick deck,
and he sailed
through the air.

"Ohhhhh," he cried as he went upward.

"Ooooooh," he cried as he came downward and saw that he was going to land on
Wendy's needle and thread, which she had
put on a barrel. Peter tried to move the
barrel aside, but it was too late. Down
came Hook, right on the needle.

"Yeeow-hoo-hoo-hoo!"

Up he went with a great howl.

And he kept going up.

Peter was so happy he crowed like a rooster. "That's a *sharp* lesson for the good captain. He always wanted to be at the top, and you can't get much higher than the mainsail yardarm!"

Wendy laughed. The pirates wanted to laugh, too, but they didn't dare.

"Come on, Wendy, let's fly back to the island. The Lost Boys will be worried about us. They like to hear your stories — and what a story you can tell them now!"

Tinker Bell's Close Call

Peter Pan's friend Tinker Bell was flying through the woods of Never Never Land when she was spied by Captain Hook. He sneaked up and got ready to grab her. "Ha, ha, Miss Clever," he sneered, "you won't get away from me now."

Tinker Bell saw the rascally pirate in time and jumped out of his reach. He chased after her, waving his sword and shouting angrily.

Tinker Bell had been drinking nectar out of the flowers, so she was heavier than usual. It slowed down her flying speed, and she couldn't escape from Hook easily. As a last resort she zipped around a big tree.

Captain Hook followed her and was surprised to find John Darling and his sister Wendy on the far side of the trunk. There was no sign of Tinker Bell — she had vanished entirely!

"Where is she?" the pirate snarled at Wendy and John. "You two must have seen her."

"Where is who?" Wendy asked with an innocent smile on her face.

"Tinker Bell,
naturally,"
bellowed Hook.
"She flew
behind this tree
a moment ago."

Wendy looked around, as if searching for Tinker Bell. "I can't see her," she said. "Can you, John?"

John got down on his hands and knees and examined the grass. "No, I can't find her, either."

The captain roared with anger and drew his cutlass. The blade gleamed in the sunlight.

"Don't try to fool me," Hook raged, waving the sword at Wendy and John. "She's here somewhere, and you're going to tell me exactly where. Speak up, or you'll be sorry!"

Wendy and John stopped smiling. They were both frightened by the pirate's threat.

Suddenly there was laughter from a tree branch overhead. "Who'll be sorry?" came a merry voice, and Peter Pan dropped from the tree to face Captain Hook.

Peter was armed
with his sword.
He pulled it out.
"I think you'll
be the one
who is sorry,
you wicked pirate,"
shouted Peter.
Captain Hook
charged at him.

"I've been waiting a long time to cross swords with you, Pan," cried Hook. "This is the end for you."

The pirate's cutlass clanged against Peter's blade again and again. Though Hook was stronger, Peter Pan was much too quick for him. The captain cried out in rage and drove his cutlass forward in a lightning thrust. Peter dodged to one side, and the point of the sword was buried in the thick bark of the tree.

Hook desperately tried to pull his cutlass from the tree trunk. Peter stepped up behind him and paddled him with the flat side of his sword. "Ouch!" yelled Hook.

"This will teach you not to bother my friends," Peter declared, spanking the unhappy pirate again.

The captain couldn't get his cutlass out of the tree, and Peter continued to paddle him. Finally Hook turned and ran away, promising to get even with Pan another day.

Peter turned to Wendy and John. "It's lucky for you two that I came along," he said. "I heard Hook ask you where Tinker Bell was. What happened to her?"

"I hid her," said John.

"Hid her? Where?"

John whipped off his top hat. "I always wear this hat, so I knew Hook wouldn't suspect that she was hiding under it."

Sure enough, there stood Tinker Bell, happily hidden where the pirate would never have thought to look — on top of John's head!

Scamp's Ball

Scamp always enjoyed walking in the park with Lady and Tramp because there were so many interesting things to see. One day they stopped to watch some tennis players. When one of them missed the ball, Tramp ran after it and caught it in his mouth.

"What's Daddy doing?" asked Scamp.

"He's getting the ball," Lady answered.

"Goody! Now we have a ball to play with," yipped Scamp.

To Scamp's surprise Tramp took the ball to the player and dropped it at her feet.

"Why, thank you," smiled the lady, patting Tramp on the head.

Scamp frowned. "Why did he do that?"

"That was the lady's ball," his mother explained. "It isn't nice to run off with something that isn't yours."

They continued on their way through the park. Ahead, two children were bouncing a red and yellow ball back and forth. A big boy came along and watched them for a moment. "That's a nice ball you've got," he grinned, grabbing it in mid-air. "I'll play with it." He kicked the ball in the air. It landed far away and rolled across the grass.

The mean boy laughed, "Ha, ha! How'd you like that kick? Pretty good, eh?"

The two little children burst out crying.

Scamp didn't think that was a nice thing for the boy to do.

Scamp dashed after the ball. However, he was so eager to get it he didn't see it bounce into a pond.

SPLASH! The ball went in the water.
SPLASH! Scamp went in after it.

The puppy promptly forgot about the ball.
All he could think about was paddling to
shore. Lady ran to the edge of the pond,
followed by Tramp. "Do something!" she
called. Tramp watched his son splashing
toward shore, working his little paws furi-
ously in a frantic dog paddle. "He's doing
fine," Tramp told Lady. "You help him onto
shore, and I'll get the ball."

Tramp jumped into the pond and swam to the ball, which was bobbing gently on the water.

Scamp reached shallow water and crawled dripping onto shore. His mother asked, "Are you all right, Scamp?"

"Sure," he gasped, shaking off the extra water.

Tramp nudged the ball forward with his nose as he swam, and soon he was on shore, too.

"See? You needn't worry,"
Tramp told Lady, smiling.
"Scamp takes after me —
he's a born swimmer."

Just then the big boy came up to snatch the ball away. Tramp began to shake himself violently, spraying cold pond water all over the boy, drenching him from head to foot. The boy ran off.

The dogs ran off to play with the two small children and their ball. Tramp said, "That big boy won't be back — he's had enough cold showers today."

Jungle Canoe

It was a warm, sunny day in the jungle — perfect for a canoe ride down the cool river. Mowgli asked Baloo to go along, but the bear declined. "I'm too big! I'd probably sink the canoe," he laughed.

So Mowgli paddled off as Baloo waved goodbye. Neither of them saw a striped figure sneaking along the shore.

The creature with the stripes was that hungry tiger, Shere Khan. However, he didn't wave goodbye to Mowgli. He didn't want Mowgli or anybody else to see him, because he planned to catch Mowgli for dinner. He scurried along the riverbank to get ahead of the canoe.

Sometimes Shere Khan was careless about his striped tail, and Baloo spotted it.

"Oh no!" gasped the big bear. "It's Shere Khan. My little buddy is in trouble!" He rushed off to try to find his friends Bagheera the panther and King Louie.

They were relaxing under a tree, unaware of Mowgli's danger. "Shere Khan's after Mowgli!" cried Baloo. "We've got to save him."

Bagheera and King Louie leaped to their feet. "Where are they?" asked the panther.

"Down the river," answered Baloo. "Mowgli's in a canoe."

Baloo said, "Hurry, Baggy. You can run faster than we can. Catch up with the tiger before he reaches Mowgli."

"Wait for me," yelled King Louie, hopping on the panther's back. Away they raced, hot on the trail of the tiger.

All this time Mowgli continued to paddle down the river, unaware of any danger.

Had Mowgli suspected something, he might have looked carefully at the big tree branches stretching over the river. Crouched on one overhanging limb was Shere Khan, waiting to pounce on Mowgli as he glided beneath.

Bagheera's keen eyes spotted the tiger. "There he is!" he whispered.

"I see him," answered Louie. "Leave him to me. I'll teach him a thing or two."

With a sudden leap and a bound, the Monkey King shot up the tree and shoved Shere Khan off the branch.

At that moment Mowgli was sliding by, and the big tiger landed in the boat. Down went the front end of the canoe and up went the rear end, flipping Mowgli high in the air!

King Louie shot out one of his long arms and caught Mowgli neatly, just like a trapeze artist in a circus. The tiger bellowed, "Yeowl!"

Mowgli found himself sitting astride the tree branch, and Shere Khan found himself in the canoe, heading downstream fast without a paddle. King Louie waved goodbye to the tiger. "Hold on tight, Shere Khan. Have a nice ride, baby!"

Shere Khan's ride was going to be anything but fun. He was heading fast for a waterfall. He went over the edge and plunged downward, landing in a deep pool.

Mowgli raced
to the pool
and managed
to rescue
the canoe
before it
was damaged.
"Shere Khan
always gets
the short end
of the stick,"
he sighed.

Shere Khan didn't answer. He was too
busy dragging his soggy self onto the opposite
bank. He crawled away as Mowgli's friends
joined him.

"Looks like Old Stripes has lost all interest
in dinner," chuckled Bagheera.

"Man, yes," said Baloo.

"I would, too," Mowgli added, "if I had
swallowed as much water as he did."

Cleaning Up

Donald Duck's three nephews loved looking at magazines, but they hated picking them up.

One day Donald went into their room and slipped on a big pile of them. He called to the boys, "Get this junk out of here."

"That isn't junk," Huey replied. "There are comic books and copies of Disneyland Magazine with stories of Pinocchio and the Jungle Book . . ."

"That's what this room looks like — a jungle," Donald said. "It's a wonder I haven't broken my back in three places and suffered a sprained beak."

Louie told his brothers, "I guess we'll never convince Unca Donald, so we'd better clean up the room."

The nephews had one more question: "Where shall we put all the comics?"

"I don't care," Donald replied. "But get them out of your bedroom."

The three boys shuffled and thumped and banged for a while, then they called to Donald, "Our room is clean now."

Donald went up to see. The room was tidy —
there wasn't a magazine in sight.

"Good boys," he said, and he gave them second
helpings of ice cream for dinner.

Donald was tired and wanted to go to bed. He
walked into his bedroom — and slipped again. There
were piles of magazines everywhere!

He called his nephews and demanded, "What are
these magazines doing here?"

"You said we could put them anywhere," said
Huey, "so we put them in *your* room!"

The Smiling Crocodile

Peter Pan was walking along the beach one day when he came face to face with a huge green crocodile. Peter knew it was the same one which frightened Captain Hook — he could tell by the tick-tocking sound that came from its stomach. (At one time the croc had gobbled an alarm clock after barely missing Captain Hook.)

"Grrowwrr," growled the crocodile. It was wild and ready to eat Peter Pan if it could.

Peter wasn't afraid.
He decided
to hypnotize
the crocodile
into being tame.
He waved his hands
and peered into
the croc's eyes.

Suddenly the crocodile sat up and smiled. Peter was proud of himself for conquering the animal so easily. He jumped on the croc's back. "I've always wanted to ride in style on the back of a smiling crocodile."

Mr. Smee,
who was spying
on Peter Pan,
was so amazed
he wanted to take
a closer look.

"Shiver me timbers!" gasped Smee. "Pan has tamed the terrible croc. Captain Hook will be so pleased."

Mr. Smee reasoned, "If the reptile is tame, the captain can get close enough to do away with it once and for all!"

He called out, "I say, Peter Pan, is that crocodile tame enough for me to take back to the ship?"

"Yes, it is. But why?" Peter asked.

Mr. Smee rubbed his nose. "The captain will be so happy to see a tame crocodile that he'll give me a reward. I'll share it with you if I can have the croc."

"What kind of reward?" asked Peter.

Smee replied,
"A tame croc
is easily worth
four quarts of
ice cream."
Peter knew Smee
was not telling
the truth.

Peter said, "Okay, it's a deal. But you mustn't hurt the crocodile."

"I wouldn't think of it," Smee replied.

He climbed on the croc's back and said, "Forward march! To the ship and a surprise for Captain Hook!"

"Now for some fun,"
thought Peter Pan.
Smee arrived at the ship
and was very excited.

"Captain Hook!" he yelled. "Look who wants to pay a friendly visit!"

"Yipes and egad!" exclaimed Hook. "The crocodile has come for me again." He didn't give Smee a chance to explain. He quickly aimed a cannon at the croc and prepared to fire.

"Goodbye, crocodile, forever!" he screamed.

BANG!

Smee tumbled off the croc's back just in time. The cannonball barely missed hitting him.

Peter Pan said to himself, "That shot from the cannon should awaken the croc from the magic spell."

The crocodile bared its many teeth, and Hook scrambled up the mast to the crow's nest. He stayed there for a week, until the crocodile went away.

Too Many Tiger Lilies

Captain Hook was ashore in Never Never Land making wicked plans. He gathered together his pirate crew and told them, "If we can capture the Indian princess, Tiger Lily, we can use her to lure Peter Pan into our clutches. I know which path she takes to visit her friends in Mermaid Lagoon, so we will lie in wait for her." The pirates nodded and grinned as they listened to their captain. "And when she least suspects it," he concluded, "ho, ho, ho . . ."

"Ho, ho, ho," went the pirates.

Captain Hook hid himself behind a palm. When Tiger Lily came along, singing happily, he jumped out!

The other pirates leaped forward, and Tiger Lily was surrounded.

"In case you don't know it, my dear, you are now my prisoner," Hook said in a silky voice.

"But why? What do you want with me? I have no money or jewels or anything," she said.

"Your friendship with Peter Pan is what we seek," said the captain. "We'll use *you* to capture *him*."

"You are a nasty pirate,"
Tiger Lily cried.
"Thank you, my dear.
Now we'll tie you to a stake
in the forest, and when Pan
comes to rescue you,
we'll swoop down
and capture him."

Hook chuckled, "And we'll make no mistake this time. My men have been practicing swoops all week."

The captain didn't see Tinker Bell watching him from the branch of a tree. She heard everything and wasted no time getting back to Peter Pan. In her own special silvery, tinkly way, she told him of Hook's plan.

"Well, I have a few tricks, too," cried Peter. "We'll have to outfox him, and if he wants to swoop, we'll give him lots to swoop at." When I get through with him he won't know whether he's swooping or swooning, winning or swimming."

Peter called the Lost Boys together and sent them to the Indian village to collect Indian dresses and feathers and moccasins. When they returned, Pan set to work disguising each boy to look like Tiger Lily.

"Up close you look nothing like Tiger Lily, but from a distance you can fool the pirates," Peter explained.

"Don't forget,"
he told them,
you musn't
be recognized
or the game is up
and Tiger Lily
might get hurt."

That evening the pirates hid near the forest clearing where Tiger Lily was tied. Suddenly Mr. Smee thought he spotted the Indian princess sneaking through the forest.

Mr. Starkey, another pirate, saw a Lost Boy in the distance. He also thought it was Tiger Lily, and he began to follow the figure in the Indian dress.

One by one, the Lost Boys fooled each of the pirates. Peter Pan watched from his perch in a tree, where he could see the clearing easily. Even Captain Hook was fooled.

All the pirates were in the woods chasing after a Lost Boy in disguise. Tiger Lily was left unguarded.

"Now's my chance," thought Peter Pan, and he glided down from his tree. He quickly cut her ropes and whispered to her, "It's me. I've come to save you from the pirates."

"Thank you, Peter.
I knew you would
rescue me,"
Tiger Lily smiled.
Peter told her,
"Now for our getaway.
Quick — to the river!"

He led Tiger Lily to the riverbank, where he had hidden a canoe. The Lost Boys ran up to join them.

"Hurry," they yelled, "Captain Hook and his pirates are not far behind."

They jumped into the canoe, and with a mighty heave Peter shoved it away from the bank into the river.

Captain Hook and his crew roared with rage when they saw all those Tiger Lilies paddle away.

Hook yelled at Smee, "You've been practicing swooping, so swoop!"

"I can't. I'll get wet," replied Smee. Hook was so angry he pushed Smee into the river. "You're all wet anyway," he said.

Peter Pan called, "You might as well give up, Hook. We're too smart for you."

The captain was so angry he pushed Mr. Starkey into the river, too.

The Stolen Kites

Wendy Darling and her brothers, John and Michael, were flying kites in the park. It was a perfect day for kites — the wind was strong and the sky was clear. Suddenly the string on Michael's kite broke, and the kite disappeared into the blue.

"Oh no," cried Michael, "I've lost my kite."

Little Michael
was very upset.
He had spent hours
making the kite.
Wendy told him,
"Cheer up!
We'll help you
make another one."

"I don't want another kite," said Michael, "I want *that* one."

Peter Pan was sitting in a nearby tree and watching everything that happened. "Don't worry, Michael," he said with a smile, "All lost kites fly to Never Never Land. We'll go to look for it." He hopped down from the tree and put his arm around Michael.

"How wonderful," the boy cried happily. "When can we go?"

"Right away," said Peter. "Do you all remember how to fly?"

The children closed their eyes and thought of a happy thought. In the wink of an eye they were speeding through the sky toward Never Never Land, the island home of Peter Pan.

Unfortunately the island was also the home of Captain Hook, the meanest pirate who ever sailed the seas.

As Peter and his friends approached the island, Peter spotted Hook's ship riding at anchor in the lagoon. He was worried.

"There's that rascal Hook prowling around looking for something to steal, no doubt," he said as they were landing.

They flew closer and saw lots and lots of gaily-colored kites tied to the mast and rigging of the ship. Peter smiled grimly to himself.

"So that's what Hook's been up to! He's been stealing kites! What a nasty thing to do," cried Peter.

Hook was indeed stealing kites. At that moment he was gleefully tying Michael's kite to the side of his ship. He cackled, "Hee, hee, this is the best kite I've caught today. I'll sell the others but keep this one for myself."

The captain was too busy gloating to notice Peter and his friends soaring above the ship. Peter grinned, "Let's have some fun with that rascal. When I say, 'Blow!' you blow with all your might."

Peter led them directly behind the ship. "All together now . . . BLOW!" he shouted. Wendy and John and Michael blew as hard as they knew how. In Never Never Land their breath was a million times more powerful than at home. Soon a storm was howling around the pirate ship.

"We'll see how Hook likes our magic wind," laughed Peter as the children continued to blow and blow.

The kites strained in the fierce wind and began to lift the ship into the sky. "Hey, put down my ship!" yelled the terrified captain.

"Anything you say, Hook," laughed Peter. He began to cut the strings of the kites.

"What are you doing?" shouted Hook.

Peter answered, "You asked me to put your ship down, didn't you?"

"No! No!" bellowed the captain. "Leave it where it is!"

"Sorry. It's too late now," Peter chuckled. With the kite strings cut, the ship was left without any support, and it fell into the sea with a tremendous splash. Peter then zipped down and took Michael's kite before the stunned captain could pick himself up from the deck.

Peter called, "Come on, everybody. Back to London."

When they were safely back in the park, Wendy asked Peter, "What would we do without you?" Peter answered, "That's simple. You'd keep on losing your kites!"

Scamp
and
the
Bullfrog

Lady and Tramp and Scamp were walking in the country, and they stopped under a shady tree to rest. Nearby a cool pond gleamed in the sunlight. Scamp thought it looked inviting, so he went exploring while his mother and father rested.

When Scamp reached the pond he heard a strange noise. "Croak! Croak!"

Scamp couldn't believe his ears. He looked around, wide-eyed.

"Croak! Croak!" Out of the reeds hopped a strange green creature with big, bulging eyes. It plopped down in front of Scamp. "Croak!"

Scamp was startled. He had never seen a bullfrog before. It looked harmless. "Uh, hi there," said Scamp. "Who are you?" "Croak! Croak!" the bullfrog said, closing its eyes. Scamp thought that the frog had gone to sleep.

The bullfrog
opened its eyes
and jumped over
Scamp's head.
It happened
so fast that
the frog
seemed
to disappear.

Scamp blinked and looked from one side to the other. "Croak!" Scamp whirled around to see the bullfrog sitting calmly, blinking its big eyes slowly. Scamp didn't know what to make of this odd green creature.

100

The bullfrog started to swell up (like frogs do when they're about to croak). It got bigger and *bigger* and BIGGER! Scamp stared in surprise. The frog puffed up until it was ready to burst.

"CROAK!" Again it jumped, heading toward the pond with great leaps.

The dog tried to imitate the frog, and he took little leaps. "Woof! Woof!" went Scamp.

"Croak! Croak!" went the frog.

The bullfrog jumped over some reeds, with Scamp right behind.

"You're not so smart," Scamp said as he jumped. "I can...GLURG!" He never finished because he fell into the pond.

Scamp came up sputtering and coughing. The green creature had tricked him again and was nowhere to be seen.

"Croak!"

Scamp couldn't see the bullfrog, mostly because it was on Scamp's head!

The frog jumped away, splashing water in Scamp's eyes. This time the creature had vanished for good. Scamp looked everywhere but couldn't find it.

Later, Tramp asked Scamp what he had seen and done to get so wet. Scamp thought about the green creature with the long legs and big eyes which croaked and could disappear in a jump. He decided Lady and Tramp would never believe him.

"I went for a swim, that's all," he said, and *this* his parents believed!

Paddling Along

Donald Duck's nephews were building a canoe, and now they were ready to launch it.

Donald watched as they carried it to the river. He wanted to be the first one to ride in it, but he knew that Huey, Dewey and Louie wouldn't let him. Donald tried hard to think of a plan which would give him the first ride.

As the nephews put the canoe in the water, Donald said, "I hear the telephone ringing in the cabin. Better go answer it, boys."

The nephews ran halfway up the path before they remembered the cabin didn't have a telephone. By this time, however, Donald was paddling the canoe in mid-river.

Donald thoroughly enjoyed himself — for a few moments. He soon found that paddling a canoe was not as easy as it looked. It was difficult to keep upright and easy to tip over. SPLASH!

Luckily for Donald, the Junior Woodchuck Guide had taught the nephews how to rescue wet uncles.

Donald sputtered, "Your canoe is no good. It keeps tipping over. I knew you'd make a mess of the job." He marched back to the cabin.

Once their uncle was out of sight, Huey and Dewey removed two heavy weights which they had hidden in one side of the canoe. Louie said, "Using those weights to make the canoe off-balance was a swell idea. Now that we've discouraged Unca Donald from using it and wrecking it, *we* can play with it."

The nephews spent the summer enjoying their canoe. Donald spent the summer trying to figure out why that canoe never did tip over again!

All in Search of a Lunch

One day Mr. Smee decided that the afternoon was so beautiful he'd serve the captain's
lunch on the deck where they could both enjoy
the sun. He took great care to fix a fine lunch
indeed. In fact, it took him so long that lunch
was very, very late.

He was ready to call the captain when the
cabin door burst open, hitting the lunch table
and knocking it overboard.

Hook roared,
"I'm hungry.
Where's lunch?"
Smee stuttered,
"Oh my, my-my,
it's out there,
in the ocean."

Smee pointed to the food, which was on the table floating toward shore.

"Smee," screamed the captain, "that's a ridiculous place to put my lunch. Fix me another."

Hook sat down to wait.

"There isn't another scrap of food on the ship," Mr. Smee answered meekly.

"I'm sorry, but you'll have to stay hungry until the other pirates return with more supplies," Smee said.

"What a dastardly turn of fate," groaned the pirate captain. He pulled out his telescope in order to keep an eye on the lunch as it drifted away. That's when he spotted something else. Someone was having a picnic on the beach.

Peter Pan was excited about bringing Wendy, John and Michael to this spot. It was a good place for a picnic and a great place to fish. They began opening their picnic basket.

Hook could tell they were having fun, and he imagined there must be a tasty, toothsome and tempting lunch in that basket.

"Hah!" laughed Hook. "I won't be hungry for long, Smee. Hurry and launch the boat. We'll make a surprise attack on Peter Pan and steal his fine lunch."

If Captain Hook could have known what was to happen, he could have saved himself some trouble!

When Wendy opened
the basket, she found
it was empty!

Wendy had remembered to pack
everything except food!

"Oh no!" moaned John.

"I'm hungry," said Michael.

"Never mind," said Peter, pointing to the ocean. "I'll catch some
fish, and we'll cook our lunch. I
always have good luck here."

Peter went to the far side of the
bay and began to fish. It wasn't long
before something tugged at his line.

"What luck!" he thought.

"I hope I can get the fish around those rocks without losing it," Peter said.

What a surprise! When Peter pulled in his line, there was Captain Hook's table with the lunch.

"Wow!" said Peter. "I've never caught anything like this with a fishing line before."

He called to the others, "Come quickly. I have a surprise for you!"

On the other side of the bay Hook and Smee were ready to charge.

Hook cried,
"They've seen us!
And the cowards
are running away!"
(He didn't know
they were running
to join Peter Pan.)

"No matter," he continued. "They've left their picnic basket. At last, a tasty lunch just for me!"

Now it was Hook's turn to be surprised. There was no food in the basket!

"Shall we go after them?" asked Smee.
"No. I'm tired and weak from hunger."

Hook sighed, "I'm so worn out I think I'll find a shady spot to rest awhile. We'll have to forget about lunch for today."

They found a cool place under a big tree, and Hook promptly fell asleep.

They didn't know the crocodile's cave was close by, and the croc was also looking for some lunch. Tick-tock. Tick-tock.

The crocodile crept close to the sleeping pirates. It had trouble sneaking up on people because of its ticking. When the croc saw that Hook was sleeping, it kept its mouth shut to muffle the tick-tocking. However, the crocodile couldn't eat lunch with its mouth closed. It was opening its big jaws when the alarm clock bell went off!

BRRRRING!

Captain Hook and Smee were so startled they almost jumped out of their skins.
Hook's teeth chattered, his knees knocked,
his arms and legs trembled — even his
hook quivered. He ran through the forest
with Smee close behind. He ran fast
enough so the crocodile went hungry, too.

The pirates ran until they came to a
clearing where Peter Pan, Tinker Bell and
the Darling children were playing hide-
and-seek.

Peter's hands
were covering
his eyes and
he was counting
while the others
tried to hide.

Peter was at sixty-two when the pirates
saw him. Hook and Smee leaped out of the
bushes and made Peter their prisoner.

"My dear Pan," smiled the pirate captain, "I've finally got you. Now to teach you
a lesson you won't forget."

Soon Tinker Bell, Wendy and the boys began to wonder where Peter was.

"Tink, do *you* know what's happened to Peter?" asked John. The pixie answered with her special fluttery, tinkling sound.

While the others waited, she went to look for Peter. She sounded like sleigh bells as she darted through the trees, searching.

Finally she spotted
Hook and Mr. Smee
forcing Peter
to go with them.
Tinker Bell became
very angry.
Her jingling sound
became a jangling,
then a jongling.

The more Tinker Bell thought about
those nasty pirates capturing Peter Pan
when he wasn't looking, the angrier she
became. When she got irritated, the
sound of her bells got lower.

Tinker Bell began sounding lower
and lower
and l
o
w
e
r

She gave an extra-heavy shrug.

BRRRRING!

Captain Hook turned white in terror. "It's the alarm clock. The crocodile is after us again. He still wants me for lunch!" In his fright Hook let go of Peter and raced for his ship. Smee wasn't far behind.

"Thanks, Tink," said Peter. "I knew I could count on you. Old Hook won't be around here for a while."

Wendy sighed with relief. "Well, I must say, that was the most exciting lunch and game of hide-and-seek I've ever had."

Jungle Hide-and-Seek

Baloo the bear's favorite game was hide-and-seek. One day he was delighted when Mowgli and Bagheera the panther asked him to play. "You bet. Can I hide first?"

"Sure," replied Bagheera. "We'll hide and Mowgli will count."

Mowgli covered his eyes and began counting to ten. "One . . . two . . . three. . . ."

Baloo called, "No peeking now, Mowgli."

Bagheera scrambled up a tree, but big, bulky Baloo had a hard time finding a tree large enough to hide him. He desperately ducked behind a narrow tree trunk, but there was more of him sticking out in front and in back than was hidden!

Poor Baloo. Mowgli spotted him right away. "One-two-three for Baloo," shouted Mowgli gleefully.

"Aw, shucks," said Baloo sadly.

"Something always goes wrong when I play hide-and-seek. I wonder what it is," the big bear groaned unhappily.

Bagheera wasn't as easy to find. He was good at hiding in trees. Mowgli looked all over but couldn't find him. "I give up, Baggy," he called. "Come out, wherever you are."

There was a rustle of leaves on the branch of a nearby tree, and the panther crawled out. Mowgli laughed, "You sure know how to hide."

"I'll bet *I* could find him," boasted Baloo.

"Okay," said Mowgli. "It's your turn to find us. Come on, Bagheera, and let's hide while Baloo counts."

They ran into the jungle. Baloo crouched on the path, wriggling with excitement. He covered his eyes and began counting slowly.

Mowgli saw a big, thick bush by the path. "Let's hide in there, Bagheera," he said. "Baloo will be looking for you up in a *tree*."

There came a clumping and thumping down the path. They peeked out to see a line of elephants led by Colonel Hathi. The patrol was making sure all was well in the jungle and that the paths were kept clear. Hathi liked to see the jungle neat and tidy.

Suddenly Hathi came upon Baloo, who was crouched on the path and counting. To Hathi Baloo looked like a big rock.

The colonel stopped so suddenly that the other elephants piled into each other like freight cars. Bump-bump-bump!

"What's this?" barked the colonel. "Who left an ugly rock in the path?"

Hathi swung his powerful trunk and swooshed Baloo away. "Hey! Help! Ooof!" yelled Baloo.

"Oh, Baloo, it's you," the colonel said. "I thought you were a rock. Dreadfully sorry. Frightful shame."

"Oh, that's all right," said Baloo.

"Nothing's gone right with this game anyway," moaned the bear.

"Game? What game?" asked the colonel.

Just then Mowgli and Bagheera came running up the path. "We were playing hide-and-seek," explained Mowgli. "Do you and your friends want to play?"

The elephants joined the game. They were so big they couldn't hide at all. Baloo always found them, so his day ended very happily.

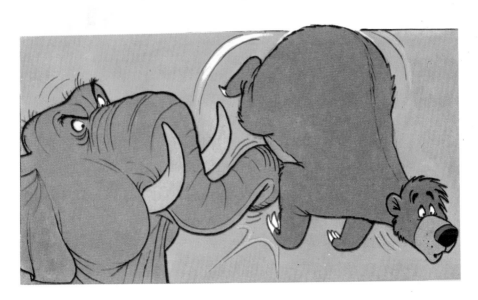

The Totem Pole

Peter Pan went to London to see a circus with John and Wendy Darling. When they returned to Never Never Land, they told the Lost Boys about the exciting things they had seen. John and Peter showed the others how the acrobats sat on each other's shoulders. After a few tumbles, they finally made it, while Wendy applauded heartily. "You should be in the circus," she laughed. "You're as good as the real acrobats."

Offshore there was another appreciative spectator. "Very clever!" sneered Captain Hook as he peered at the acrobats through his spyglass. He turned to his first mate, Mr. Smee, "Let's upset their little act," he said, grinning evilly.

Smee grinned back just as evilly. He aimed the ship's cannon at the boys and touched a flame to the firing hole.

BOOM! A cannonball screamed through the air right past the boys.

All the boys lost their balance and tumbled into the sand. "Ho, ho, ho," Captain Hook guffawed, gazing through his spyglass.

"That's a funny act," Hook said. "If I shoot another cannonball maybe they'll do an encore!"

Peter and the boys picked themselves up, brushing off the sand and rubbing the sore spots where they had hit the ground. "That was a nasty trick," muttered John.

"Never mind," Peter said quietly. "I know how we can pay back old Hook." Then he shouted so Hook could hear, "Come on, boys! Let's go and practice our act where that mean old Captain Hook can't bother us."

Hook watched, a big grin on his face, as Peter went inland with the boys and Wendy. "So Peter thinks he's smart, does he? Smee, get the cannon ashore. We'll follow them."

Peter led his friends to the Indian camp, where Tiger Lily greeted them. "What brings you to our village, Peter?" she smiled.

"We've come to see that new totem pole your father is carving."

The Big Chief was delighted to show off his new totem pole. "Can we see how it looks standing up?" asked Peter.

"Sure," nodded the Big Chief.

They pushed and pulled
to stand up
the totem pole.

"Hey, it looks just like us doing our acrobat act," laughed John.

"Why, so it does," Peter replied, winking at Wendy.

She thought, "Oh oh, Peter's up to something."

Hook and Smee, who was dragging the cannon, trailed Peter and his friends to the Indian camp. As they sneaked up, Hook saw the totem pole silhouetted against the sky. "Ha! They've gone into their act again. Let 'em have it, Smee!"

BOOM!

The cannon roared and another cannonball screamed through the air. When the smoke cleared, Hook saw to his amazement that the boys were not scared by the shot, for they were still standing. "Let 'em have another one, Smee," he yelled, "and this time don't you dare miss!"

"I-I only brought one shot," stammered Smee.

"Idiot!" screamed Hook, dashing his hat to the ground. "Do I have to do everything myself?" In a rage he ran forward to tackle the balancing boys.

He crashed through some bushes and thudded into the totem pole, which fell over with a crash that shook the entire village.

"Oooh, I hurt my nose," moaned Hook as he sat on the ground in a daze. The Big Chief glared at him, pulled out his tomahawk and advanced toward Hook. "That isn't all that's going to hurt when I get through," he roared.

Hook scrambled
to his feet
and began to run
from the village.
Smee followed,
dragging
the cannon.
The Chief was
close behind.

Peter and his friends watched with delight as the Big Chief chased Hook and Smee into the ocean, where they swam frantically toward their ship. John laughed, "That's funny. Hook should be in the circus."

"Right," chuckled Peter. "However, I don't think old Hook will want to repeat *that* act!"

Secret of Green Cave

Peter Pan was seated near a campfire telling stories. When he finished, his audience (the Lost Boys and John and Michael Darling) didn't want to leave.

"Tell us about your hidden treasure," John insisted.

"All right," he replied. He was about to make up a story about some treasure when he heard Tinker Bell. She flew to his shoulder to get his attention.

By fluttering her wings and pointing, she made Peter understand that Captain Hook was hiding behind a tree and could hear everything Peter was saying.

"Thanks, Tink," Peter whispered. He knew he could always rely on her when danger threatened. Peter said to himself, "Let me see. How can I teach Hook a lesson?"

He had an idea, and he pretended he didn't know the pirate was nearby.

"I was going to tell you about my treasure," Peter said in a loud voice. "Well, as you know, it's hidden in Green Cave."

The boys had no idea
Hook was lurking nearby.
They were startled
to hear footsteps
running into the woods.
"What was that?"
they asked.
"Captain Hook,"
Peter answered.
"Tinker Bell warned me
he was listening.
I think we've tricked
him good this time."

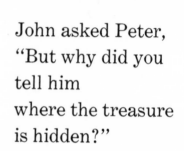

John asked Peter,
"But why did you
tell him
where the treasure
is hidden?"

"You'll see," Peter replied.

He jumped to his feet and motioned the boys to follow him. "Let's get to Green Cave before the captain does."

Peter took a short cut to the cave. They barely had time to hide themselves before Hook came sneaking down the trail.

"Ho, ho, ho. This is my big chance to get Peter Pan's treasure," he chuckled, slipping into the dark cave.

"Wait another minute," Peter said, "and you'll see what happens when Captain Hook finds the surprise waiting for him!"

Suddenly, from deep within the cave, there came a horrible yell!

"YEEEOW!"

Captain Hook was racing from the cave. Nipping at his heels was the crocodile!

Peter and the boys roared with laughter as Hook ran down the trail toward the safety of his pirate ship. The crocodile chased after him, tick-tocking all the way, and clicking its huge teeth hungrily.

"The crocodile was part of my treasure that Hook didn't expect to find," laughed Peter.

Walking the Plank

John and Michael Darling were in Never Never Land playing with the Lost Boys when they were spied by that villain, Captain Hook.

"Aha," sneered Hook, "I think I'll take those boys prisoner and make them walk the plank! There's nothing better to brighten an afternoon than a good plank-walking."

With that, he sent his biggest and burliest crewman ashore to capture the boys. When the children saw the pirates coming, they tried to run away, but they weren't fast enough. Within an hour they were tied hand and foot to the ship's mast.

"How delightful!"
cried the captain.
"This afternoon
we'll have ourselves
a jolly plank-walking.
Smee, I want these boys
to have five portions
of chocolate cake each."

Hook laughed to himself, "All that choco-late cake in their bellies will send 'em to the bottom even faster!"

As Smee fed
the children,
Hook chuckled,
"Captain Hook always
takes care of his guests."

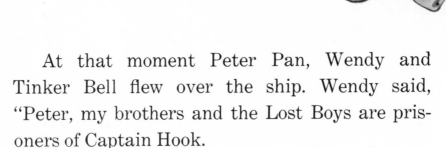

At that moment Peter Pan, Wendy and Tinker Bell flew over the ship. Wendy said, "Peter, my brothers and the Lost Boys are prisoners of Captain Hook.

"Follow me," cried Peter, heading toward the ship. "I'm going to free them."

They were
on the deck
in an instant.
She couldn't
loosen the knots.
Peter's sword
couldn't cut
any of the
stout ropes.

Wendy sobbed, "Peter, what are we going to do now?"

"I'll think of something," he said. Suddenly he heard a sail flapping , and he looked up. "I've got it. I know what to do! Quick, Wendy, I need help!"

First Peter moved the plank to the other side of the ship. Then he released the anchor line for a few minutes. "It's a good thing Hook and Smee are below decks preparing for the afternoon's ceremony, otherwise we'd be in bad trouble."

Off they flew to the beach, with Peter assuring Wendy that her brothers would be saved.

An hour later
Captain Hook
watched Smee
untie the boys.
"Hurry up,"
he growled.

When the boys were free, Hook said, "I want the prisoners to walk the plank right now!"

"Aye, sir," said Smee, herding the boys toward the plank.

Neither Hook nor Smee
noticed that the plank
was now on the opposite
side of the ship.
They also failed to see
that the ship had moved
and was no longer
in the middle of the bay.

"Overboard you go, lads," shouted Hook.

One by one the boys walked to the end of the plank and jumped off. Amazingly, not one of them fell in the water. Instead, they landed on the beach, where Peter Pan and Wendy were waiting for them.

Captain Hook was outraged when he saw them running away. "I'll get you yet," he thundered after Peter.

Peter Pan shouted from a distance, "I loosened the anchor line so the wind blew the ship to the beach, and I switched the plank to the shore side. It's the *only* way to walk the plank!"

The Birdman

There was trouble in Never Never Land. Captain Hook had captured Tinker Bell!

He took her into his cabin and locked her in a birdcage. She tried to signal to Peter Pan for help, but this time the evil captain was too smart for her. "You'll stay locked in that birdcage, Miss Bell," said Hook with an oily smile, "and soon Peter Pan will be my prisoner."

The captain planned to capture Peter by using Tinker Bell as a decoy. He wasn't yet certain exactly how his plan would work, so he went ashore to think it out. As he strode down the gangplank Hook muttered to himself, "This time I'll win! I'll get the better of Pan for sure."

Hook wouldn't have been so confident if he'd known that Mr. Smee was entering his cabin at that very moment. Smee was first mate on the ship (first at the dinner table and first in stupidity). He was also very nearsighted.

"Oh, a little bird,"
said Smee as he spotted
Tinker Bell in the cage.

"How nice of the captain to bring a bird aboard our ship," Smee added to himself. He was so nearsighted he didn't recognize that the "bird" was Tinker Bell, and he didn't see Peter Pan staring in the window. (Peter had heard Tinker Bell's tinkle for help and had rushed to the ship to aid her.)

Smee settled into Hook's favorite chair and fell asleep. A short time later, Smee awoke to hear a voice calling from shore:

"New birds for old! New birds for old! I'm the birdman of Never Never Land."

Smee jumped up and ran to the window. He saw a strange old fellow with a long white beard standing on the beach. "What do you want?" Smee asked.

"I trade new birds for old ones. Can we make a deal?"

The man held a cage and inside was a big parrot. Smee gazed at Hook's tiny cage with the little bird.

Smee hurried to shore to take a better look at what the birdman was offering.

"My, what a fine big bird!" he said.

The old man replied, "No pirate ship should be without a parrot. This is a fine bird. Wings hardly used at all — only to fly to the supermarket once a week. Guaranteed thirty miles to the pound of birdseed."

The birdman added,
"Look at these
two-tone feathers
and the solid beak —
a sign of quality.
Now, the problem
is this: What have
you got to trade?"

Smee said, "I don't have any old *big* birds, but I do have a sparkling little bird."

"Well, I don't know. There's not much market for little birds these days, even ones that sparkle," the birdman answered.

"Let me get it and show it to you," Smee suggested.

"Well, all right," said the birdman. Smee raced to the ship, picked up Tinker Bell's cage, and ran to shore.

The birdman agreed to trade.

Smee was very happy. "The captain is sure to be pleased when he sees this fine big bird I've traded for that silly little one!"

Hook returned in time to see the old man with Tinker Bell remove his beard and disguise. It was Peter Pan!

Hook raged, "Peter Pan has rescued Tinker Bell!" He raced aboard his ship. Smee couldn't wait to tell him what a clever trade he'd made. Hook wouldn't listen. He just glared at the parrot, which bit him on the nose!

The new parrot not only bit Captain Hook, but it never stopped talking!

High Diving Duck

A new swimming pool was being built in the park near Donald Duck's house. It was an Olympic size pool with three diving boards at the deep end! When Donald heard about the diving boards, he said, "I'm the best diver in the world. You'll be amazed when you see me going off that high board."

On opening day everyone went to the pool, and the crowd waited for Donald to dive.

Donald climbed the steps. Up — *up* — UP! The ground was very far away. He walked out on the board. All eyes were on him.

"Gulp! Ulp!" he choked as he looked down at the water, about a hundred miles below him. The board was lots higher than he thought.

"I can't dive off here," gasped Donald. "I wouldn't do a swan dive — it would be a *dead-duck* dive!"

He looked at all the people watching him and thought, "Oh boy, I'd better do something."

He leaned over the rail and called, "Just a minute!"

He climbed down the board, ran to his garage and returned with a rope ladder hidden under the top of his swimsuit.

Up the board climbed Donald Duck. He bowed to the crowd on the left and on the right. He saluted the flag flying ahead of him.

Quickly he tied the rope to the board and climbed down into the water.

The audience shouted, "Cheat! Faker! Bum!"

"No," Donald replied with confidence. "I said you would be amazed when you saw how I went off the high board. Well, you *were* amazed, weren't you?"

Peter Saves Wendy

Captain Hook was singing as he headed for his ship. He was singing so loudly he awakened the crocodile. The croc began swimming toward Hook, tick-tocking all the while. Hook didn't hear the clock ticking until the last moment — the croc's big teeth were nearly closed on the pirate's coattails. "E-e-e-eyow!" screamed Hook, leaping high in the air.

Hook ran
headlong
into the jungle.
The pirate was
so frightened
he didn't stop
for three miles.

"Phew," he gasped. "That was a narrow escape." Just then he heard a noise. "It's that crocodile again," he thought, ducking behind a tree to hide.

He peeked to see what the noise was. His eyes sparkled when he saw it was Wendy Darling.

"What luck," he thought. "I'll capture her and tell Peter Pan I'll release her only if he surrenders himself to me!" When Wendy passed by, he jumped in front of her.

"Got you!" he shouted. "You are my prisoner! But I won't hurt you if you'll help me capture Peter Pan!"

"Never! Peter is my best friend, and I'll never let you hurt him," she said.

"Then you'll sit here until you change your mind," said Hook, tying her up.

Watching all of this was Tinker Bell. She flew to Peter Pan and found him taking a nap. She awakened him and in her silvery, fluttery, tinkly manner told him that Wendy was in trouble.

"I must save her," said Peter. "But how?" Then he got an idea.

Hook was threatening Wendy with his sword. "I'll give you five minutes to say you'll help me or I'll . . ."

Hook heard a loud ticking. His face turned green with fright. "Yow!" he yelled. "The crocodile. He's come back for the rest of me!" Hook spun on his heels and raced away for dear life. He ran for the safety of his ship as fast as he could, which was pretty fast.

As he vanished, Wendy heard Peter Pan chuckle. He stepped from his hiding place.

"It was you," cried Wendy. "I thought it was the crocodile."

"So did Hook," Peter said merrily. "That's why I brought my alarm clock with me."

Jungle Rain Dance

It had been raining long and hard, even for the jungle. Mowgli and his two best friends, Bagheera the panther and Baloo the bear, sat under a palm tree glumly watching the rain.

"Will it ever stop raining?" sighed Mowgli.

"I wish I knew," replied Bagheera. "Rain makes me feel wet and miserable."

"Me, too," added Baloo.

The raindrops beat steadily on the palm fronds overhead. "Sounds like a drum roll," Bagheera remarked.

"Drum roll?" exclaimed Baloo, as a big drop plopped on his nose. "That reminds me.

Do you know that in some places people do special dances to bring on the rain?"

"So who needs more rain?" grumbled the panther.

"That's the point. Why not have a dance to turn the rain *off?*"

Bagheera frowned. "Hmmm. Sort of an *anti*-rain dance?"

"Sure," said Baloo brightly. "What have we got to lose?" The bear grabbed Mowgli and pulled him into the rain.

"Get with the beat,
Little Britches,
and we'll make up
a go-away rain dance!"

"Why not?" laughed Mowgli. "We can't get any wetter than we are!"

Off they danced, sloshing through puddles. Baloo held a palm frond as an umbrella, which did no good at all. He sang, "Rain, rain, go away. Come again another day." The rain came down harder, but they kept on dancing and singing.

They splashed their way to the old ruins, where King Louie lived. They heard a deep voice from within.

"Who's monkeying around out there?"

"Me and Mowgli," shouted Baloo. "We're dancing the rain away."

King Louie looked out and guffawed when he saw Baloo and Mowgli in the mud. "It's raining harder than ever. Whoever's sending down the rain sure doesn't dig your dancing."

"Maybe you can do better?" called Baloo. "Or are you afraid of getting your royal feet wet, king-baby?"

"I'll show you, you blow-hard bear!" King Louie yelled.

Louie leaped off the wall
and called to his flunkeys,
"Start the beat!"

Three monkeys picked up their clubs and
began tapping out a tattoo on their log tom-
toms. Thoomp! Thoomp! Thoomp! The sound of
the drums drowned out the sound of the rain.
Baloo and King Louie joined hands and whirled
faster and faster. If nothing else, the bear and
the monkey loved dancing!

Mowgli looked up toward the sky. "Hey, the rain has stopped!" he shouted. And he was right.

The dark rain clouds were moving away, and sunlight flooded the jungle.

The rain had stopped, but King Louie hadn't. Once he started dancing, he couldn't stop. He whirled even faster. He let go of Baloo's hand.

WHOOSH! The bear flew into the bushes. A moment later came another sound. SPLASH!

Bagheera ran up. "You did it!" he cried happily to Mowgli. "You really stopped the rain."

"You'd better believe it, man," said King Louie proudly.

Bagheera looked around. "Where's Baloo?" he asked.

Mowgli replied, "He flew off into the bushes."

The two friends found Baloo sitting calmly in a pool of water, a big smile on his face. "Man, this is great," grinned Baloo.

"Haven't you been wet enough today?" snorted Bagheera.

"This is different. This is a cool pool."

The panther and the boy would never quite understand their big furry friend. But as long as he was happy, that was what counted!

Over the Rainbow

"I wish I could do that," John Darling said as he listened to Peter Pan play a tune on his musical pipe.

"You could if you tried hard enough," said Peter. "It takes lots of practice. And this is a special pipe. It's for Wendy. I'll play it at her surprise birthday party we're giving today."

"Yippee!" yelled the Lost Boys.

They wouldn't have been so happy if they had known Captain Hook and Mr. Smee were spying on them from the bushes.

"Look at that," exclaimed Hook. "The music from that pipe is so sweet that even the animals are coming to listen."

"I've never seen anything like it," Smee answered. "This music is enchanting the rabbits and squirrels, and even a wild turkey has come out of hiding."

"Turkey?" questioned Hook. "Hmmm. That gives me an idea. We haven't had a turkey dinner for a long time. What an easy way to catch one of those birds."

"How's that?" asked Smee.

"Think, man. All I have to do is make a pipe, play on it, and when a wild turkey comes to hear my tune, we catch it and roast it for dinner."

Hook carved himself a pipe, and when it was finished he tried to blow on it. Bleep! Bloop! Squeek! Toot! Blat! "Ahh," sighed Hook, taking a breath, "the sound of sweet music."

Mr. Smee didn't agree. He put his fingers in his ears so he couldn't hear the terrible noise.

Smee said meekly, "Captain, I think you need some practice. You don't know how to play that pipe." "Nonsense!" Hook replied. "I can play as well as Pan. See that turkey over there behind the rock?"

Smee couldn't believe his eyes, but it looked like some dumb turkey had come to listen to Hook's awful music.

The two pirates crept toward the rock and pounced.

What a surprise!

It wasn't a turkey after all!

It was the Indian Chief!

What Hook had seen was the feathered headdress of the Big Chief, who had been napping behind the rock.

The Big Chief was in a rage. He called for his braves and made the pirates his prisoners. "No one wakes me up and gets away with it. You will be punished," he scowled.

The punishment was to serve the food and to entertain at Wendy's birthday party. Wendy loved seeing Hook try to sing and dance and play the pipes. When Mr. Smee messed up "Chopsticks" on the piano, everybody laughed.

The best thing about the party, however, was the rainbow that appeared at the end.

"Oh, isn't it pretty?" said Wendy. "The sun is catching the mist just right."

"I've never seen such a bright rainbow," said John. "See how the colors range from red to orange, yellow, green, blue and violet?"

"Those are the colors all right," said Peter. "And remember, they are always in that order — red, orange, yellow, green, blue and violet."

Little Michael said, "Let's try to climb it and find the pot of gold at the end of the rainbow."

"It's no use,"
Peter explained.
"The closer you get
to a rainbow,
the farther it
moves away."

The rainbow had given Captain Hook another evil idea. "If the boys want to climb a rainbow, we'll build a special one with a trap at the end!" The pirates all chuckled at the scheme.

When the Indians set Hook free, he ordered his men to build a rainbow out of wood. It disappeared into the tops of the trees. Hook said, "I can't wait to get my hands on those boys. When they are my prisoners, Peter Pan will do anything I say."

Soon the children came along. John exclaimed, "Look, there's another rainbow. And it isn't moving away from us."

"Let's climb it and find the pot of gold," cried Michael. The two boys happily scrambled up the wooden rainbow.

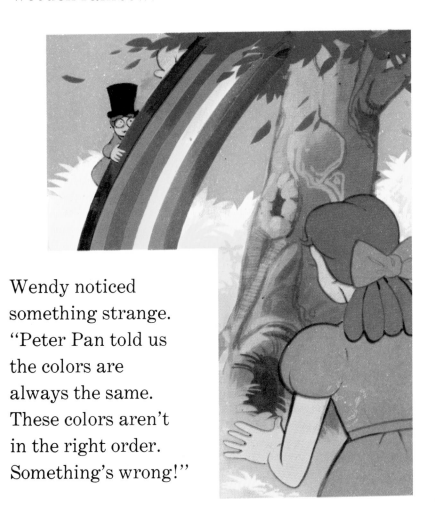

Wendy noticed something strange. "Peter Pan told us the colors are always the same. These colors aren't in the right order. Something's wrong!"

Wendy hurried to find Peter Pan. When he heard about the new rainbow, he flew there as fast as he could. He arrived as John and Michael were falling off the end of it into a big net Captain Hook held to catch them.

"Help!" shouted little Michael. Down swooped Peter. He caught the boys before they landed in the net.

"Blast you, Peter Pan," screamed an angry Captain Hook.

The pirates watched helplessly as Pan flew the boys to safety.

Pan also kicked a can of yellow paint so it landed on Hook's head. He laughed, "There's the pot at the end of the rainbow!"

Wendy's Clothesline

Wendy Darling had a huge basket of laundry to wash. It belonged to the Lost Boys in Never Never Land, but there was so much that she took it to London, where there was more hot water and soap.

"There's too much laundry. I don't have enough clothesline to hang it out to dry." she sighed. "What can I do?"

"Why not divide the job in two?" John suggested. "Do half today and half tomorrow."

Little Michael said, "Why not simply get a longer rope?"

"That's a good idea," said Wendy, so they went to the store and bought a new clothesline. On the way back, they heard what sounded like a sword fight in the park.

There was shouting and yelling, too. Wendy thought she recognized the voices.

"I don't like the sound of this," she said, trying to peer through the heavy shrubbery into a clearing.

"It's fighting all right," said Michael.

The noise grew louder as the battle got worse. "We'd better stop it before someone gets hurt," said an alarmed Wendy. "Follow me."

They all ran
to the clearing
and what they saw
shocked them.
Peter Pan
and Captain Hook
were dueling.
Hook snarled,
"I knew if I
got you away from
Never Never Land
and away from
your magic
that I'd defeat
you at last!"

Peter and Hook were chasing each other around the clearing and jabbing with their swords. The metal clanged loudly when the swords crossed.

"Take that, you scurvy brat," yelled Hook as he slashed at Peter.

"Missed me," Peter replied, dancing away from the flashing sword.

"Stop this instant!"
yelled Wendy Darling,
stamping her foot.
But they paid no attention.

Suddenly Peter Pan stumbled and fell. Captain Hook was over him instantly, pointing his sword at Pan's throat. "I've got you at last. I've waited a long time to get even with you," snarled Hook.

Wendy gasped, "We've got to save Peter, but how?"

John snatched the clothesline. "I know how to save him." He ran to a nearby tree.

Michael gave John a boost, and the boy shinnied up the tree.

Out of the corner of his eye Peter saw what was happening and began to crawl backwards away from Hook.

John climbed onto a thick branch.

"You can't escape this time," Hook sneered. "When I count three, you'll get yours, Peter Pan."

Hook waved
his sword
and stepped
closer
to Peter.
The captain
began to count.
"One . . . Two . . ."
John edged
along the limb
until he
was above
Captain Hook.
He formed
a lasso
with the rope
and dropped it
on Hook's hook.
Then he pulled
the rope tight.
Hook was yanked
off the ground.